F
W213i

I Have a Question, God

Jeannette W. Ward

BROADMAN PRESS
Nashville, Tennessee

T 6028

© Copyright 1981 • Broadman Press
All rights reserved.

ISBN: 0-8054-4265-0
4242-65

Dewey Decimal Classification: CE
Subject heading: ADOPTION-FICTION

Library of Congress Catalog Card Number: 80-70521

Printed in the United States of America

To

Mother and Dad who gave me life,

Bill who gave my life purpose,

and Wendi and Traci who gave OUR lives meaning

I have a question, God. I need your help. At times I feel like nobody loves me, but I know they do. I know you love me, God. Mom and Dad do too. Even Rusty, my pesky kid brother, loves me. Grandmother Griffin has always loved me. She thinks there's no one like her Sandi. That's what everybody calls me. But God, you know my real name is Sandra, don't you? I think my friend Beth likes me, too, but sometimes I'm not sure. See, she's like a seesaw. One day she likes me, the next day she doesn't. Even grouchy Mrs. Applebonham, that fourth-grade teacher I had last year, sometimes acted as if she thought I were nice. I guess I believe all this God—except on days when I'm wondering.

I remember when we moved from Florida to Villa Ridge, that tiny town in Virginia. I hated it even though I was only five then. I'm almost grown now. Mom says I'm eleven going on fifteen. The only time I had fun then was when it snowed. How I'd miss the snow and Mom's snow ice cream. It's neat! She puts green food coloring and peppermint flavoring in it. Once she used fresh orange juice.

My friend Lisa and her family moved to Virginia at the same time. Our fathers worked for the same company. Lisa hated those winter days too. She didn't have a sister or brother either, so we played together often.

One day Lisa and I were upstairs in my bedroom playing. Lisa said, "Hey, Sandi, did you know Mrs. Benson is going to have a baby?"

I didn't want Lisa to think she knew more than I did, especially since Mrs. Benson was my next-door apartment neighbor. So I said, "Sure, I know it. One day she is going to lean over like this [and I bent forward from my waist], and plop, out will come the baby." When I was five, that's how I thought babies were born.

We watched Mrs. Benson's stomach grow bigger and bigger. We sometimes played doctor. Lisa and I took turns pretending to be Mrs. Benson and the doctor.

God . . . I guess watching Mrs. Benson's stomach grow is what first started my wondering. You know what I mean, God. Wondering how babies are made and where they come from.

I had been thinking about this baby stuff. Once when Mom and I were riding home from kindergarten, I just blurted out, "Mom, did I grow inside you?"

She smiled and said, "No, Sandi, you grew inside another mommy. But I'll be your mother forever!"

That seemed sort of strange, but it was OK with me because I know Mom loves me. She is always around to patch a skinned knee, wipe tears, and color pictures. Soon we were talking about what had happened that morning at kindergarten. I forgot about babies and where they come from.

I forgot until one day this girl who lived in a nearby apartment thought she had the world's biggest secret to tell. Her name was Debra.

Debra and I were playing mommy and daddy. She leaned over to me and whispered, "Sandi, I hate to tell you this, but you're adopted. I grew inside my mother and you didn't."

I knew I was adopted. Mom and Dad had called me their *precious adopted child* for as long as I could remember. "So what smartie? I know it," I said.

Debra was sort of pretty. Dark eyes, long black hair, and dark skin. But boy, was she bossy. She thought she knew everything. She wasn't exactly my best friend. But when Lisa couldn't play, I liked to play with Debra.

Remember that night, God? After Mom read my bedtime story, I said my prayer. I asked you why I didn't grow inside Mom like Debra grew in her mother. Mom didn't know what Debra had told me. A funny look came on her face. She said, "Sandi, why did you ask God that?"

I'd been wanting to know more about this ever since Debra told me.

Mom snuggled me close and explained, "It's

7

true that Debra grew inside her mother. She was born into her family. That is *one* way of becoming a family. However, her parents were unable to choose between a boy or girl. We especially wanted a little girl like you. We talked to some trained people who could help us. After what seemed like a long wait, we became an adoptive family.

"Something unusual and exciting happened to us that day. You and I went to *your own* baby shower that same night. It just worked out that way," Mom said.

It wasn't many days until Debra and I were playing mommy and daddy again. She said, "Sandi, remember what I told you about being adopted?"

I pretended not to remember. "What?"

"You know, about growing inside my mother and you didn't."

"Now was my chance," I thought. "Yeah, your mother and father had to take what grew inside her. My mother and father asked for me." I guess that hushed Miss Big Mouth. That was my name for Debra when I was mad, but she didn't know it.

But God, sometimes I remember what Debra said. And what Mom told me when I asked if I grew inside her. When I was in the first grade, I

began to wonder about my first mother. I started wondering more. I still remember that day . . .

One Sunday morning, Dad and I were ready for church and waiting in the car for Mom. "Dad, why did that lady give me away?" I asked.

Patting me on the head, he smiled and said, "I'm sure it was for a good reason. Maybe she couldn't give you a comfortable home, enough food and clothes, or other things she wanted her baby to have. Mom and I wanted a baby like you, so now we are a family. We will be a family always."

Mom came to the car, wearing a pink dress that was my favorite. We went to church. Nothing else was said about my first mother until that evening. Dad and I were sitting in his big green chair, watching television and munching popcorn. When the program was over, Dad said, "Sandi, do you want to talk about your first mother some more?"

I said, "No, but tell me the story of Sandi again." So he did.

Mom first told me the story of Sandi when I was very little. It seemed to me that being adopted is something great. I always liked hearing about Sandi.

One day Dad came home from work, crossed his arms, and leaned against the kitchen sink. He asked Mom and me, "How would you like to move to a big city in Virginia?" I was still in first grade.

There wasn't much to do in Villa Ridge, but I had begun to like it. I was sad about leaving my pretty first-grade teacher and the steep hill that we zipped down on our bikes. Lisa had already moved back to Florida, so I was over missing her. But I was a little sad about leaving Debra.

A big, yellow and green moving van with a yellow ship painted on its side backed up to our apartment. Four men jumped out, rushed inside, and began loading. Dishes, clothes, my toys, furniture—everything!

We had already rented a pretty apartment in Sommerville. It had bright rust carpet. A closet in my bedroom was large enough to be a small playroom. Mom thought having such big closets was neat.

Our apartment was close to the swimming pool. They had a swim team too. For someone like me who loves to swim, well, that sure made me happy.

Soon I met two girls who lived in the same apartment building. Their names were Shelia and Greta. We became friends. I didn't much like Greta because she reminded me of Debra. Shelia and I became the kind of friends that are like cooked oatmeal—instant and stuck together. We joined the swim team. Shelia could swim faster than I could. Probably because she had a big brother to teach her. I didn't mind that. We had fun racing against one another for practice.

The night before a swim meet Mom would say, "Sandi, eat lots of meat tonight. It will give you energy that will stay with you overnight. Just before the swim meet tomorrow, eat Jell-o for quick energy." It must have worked. That summer I won six blue ribbons for first place and four red ones for second. Our team even came in second in the championship meet.

That was a happy summer for me, God. But somehow my wondering kept sneaking back. I just don't understand why they gave me away. Occasionally I'd look at myself in the bathroom mirrow. "I'm not the prettiest girl in the world, but I'm sure not the ugliest," I'd think. So it can't be because they were ashamed of how I looked. Sometimes, God, I feel so alone. Do all kids feel this way?

I used to say, "Boy, I wish I had a sister or brother."

When I was in second grade, I cried and asked Mom, "Please get me a sister or brother. Let's find a little child who needs a home and adopt it."

Mom asked me questions like, "Would you rather have a baby sister or brother? Or would

you rather have one big enough to play with?"
Babies are sweet, but I wanted *someone* to play
with.

It was a fast summer. A few weeks before
school started, we moved to a white brick house
with green siding. This time we lived out of the
city. Mom was so happy. She said, "This is just
what I've always wanted. Plenty of closets, a
fireplace, and enough yard for a garden."

Dad wasn't very excited about cutting grass. He
soon bought a bright orange garden tractor. He
told Mom, "Now I can cut grass and plow *your*
garden too."

I missed my friends from the apartment.
Thoughts of not being on the swim team next
year made me sad.

When we moved into our house, Mom was
upstairs unpacking boxes. The doorbell rang. I
opened the door. There stood a girl about my
age.

"Hi, I'm Susan, from across the street. What's
your name?"

"Sandi," I told her.

"Can you ride bikes with me?"

"Let me ask my mom." I was so excited I
skipped every other step going upstairs.

"Mom, Susan wants me to ride bikes with her.
May I go?"

"Who?" called Mom, raising her head up out of
a box.

"Susan, from across the street. Please, Mom?"

"OK, but don't go far until we learn more about the neighborhood," she cautioned. She's always cautioning me about something. Mothers are like that I suppose.

Susan introduced me to some kids. A boy who lived next door to Susan came slouching out of his house with his hands hanging out of his pants pockets by his thumbs. He walked toward us. I thought he might be practicing for a quick-draw scene in a Western movie the way he was swinging his body first to the left and then to the right, kicking every rock in his path.

"Jeff, this is Sandi. Sandi, this if Jeff," said Susan.

I played with Susan and Jeff a lot during the summer. Although Jeff and I got along, I didn't feel comfortable around him. He was always getting into a fight with some of the kids. When anyone disagreed with him, he would make a face and mutter something like, "What are you going to do about it?" He also liked the sound of words I wasn't supposed to say.

I was glad when school started. I made new friends. And I made excuses so I didn't have to play with Jeff.

God, I hope that wasn't wrong. You know, making excuses not to play with Jeff. He was always nice to me. But I didn't like the way he

14

bullied some of the other kids around, especially boys smaller than he was. Besides, I didn't like to listen to his bad language. I know you agree with that, don't you, God?

For the first time in my life, I rode a real, honest-to-goodness, yellow school bus. Sometimes though it wasn't much fun. Especially when I had to sit beside a boy and the other kids teased me.

It was just my luck to get Mrs. Applebonham that year for my teacher. If she ever smiles, I bet her face will crack.

God, Mrs. Applebonham made me want to crawl under my desk. I also began wondering about myself again. Seems like my questions get bigger and bigger.

Fall came and then winter. One night Dad and Mom were downstairs in the den talking. The fire was burning. The flames were like a ballet. Dad and Mom called me to come downstairs. I could tell by the looks on their faces that something was up.

Dad held me in his lap. Mom was sitting nearby. She had her dying-to-tell-something look on her face.

Dad said, "Sandi, remember when you were in second grade and begged Mom to get a sister or brother for you? Remember Mrs. Alden, the

social worker who visited us and talked to us about helping us find another child who would be your sister or brother?"

I thought to myself, "Boy, something strange is going on!" I hadn't answered Dad's question, so I nodded my head. "Yes."

"How would you like a brother? One old enough to play with you?"

Every time they do something special for me, that's exactly the way Dad talks. "How would you like . . . ?" I knew they must have a brother for me. But where was he?

Then Mom handed me a picture of a little boy. He was wearing brown slacks and a yellow and brown plaid shirt. He was sitting on somebody's sofa. He looked about five or six years old. He was cute. Reddish-brown hair, a few freckles, brown eyes, and a shy smile.

His name is Russell, but everyone calls him Rusty Mom and Dad told me. He would be my new brother.

"We will have to wait about two weeks before we can meet him," Mom said. "He has an ear infection." They told me Rusty was living in a temporary home, waiting for a forever home.

I carried his picture to school the next day and showed it to my friends, teachers, and the principal. I even got up courage to show it to Mrs. Applebonham. She *almost* smiled.

That was two long weeks. Mom and I

decorated Rusty's bedroom. His curtains and bedspread were blue with white stars to go with the red carpet. His room looked like a flag.

Finally it was time to meet Rusty. We got up early to take the long trip. Mom explained that Rusty would be frightened. We might have to visit him a few times before he would be ready to come home with us. Mom wasn't exactly correct. After Rusty got over being afraid of us, we toured a big battleship and then went to the beach. Rusty was fun to play with at the beach. We stayed in a high-rise motel by the ocean. It reminded me of the apartment by the ocean in Florida where we used to live. Rusty's social worker brought along his sleeping bag. Mom had packed mine. They thought it might be fun for us to sleep in them that night. Rusty began talking while unrolling his sleeping bag. Much later I fell asleep. Rusty was still talking. Rusty was ready to go home with us the next day.

But something happened that day in the motel, I'll never forget. Rusty and I got into an elevator. Rusty had not been on many elevators. When it stopped, I got off. Rusty waited too long. The door shut before Rusty could get out. Just as the door closed I yelled, "Rusty, punch number four!" I ran to our room. I told Mom and Dad and the lady from the adoption agency what had happened. They came out of the room like the motel was on fire.

Mom dashed into an elevator. She went from floor to floor trying to find Rusty. No one seemed to care that I was scared. What seemed like hours later, a maid stepped off the elevator on the fourth floor. Rusty was holding her hand. He looked frightened. Mom grabbed Rusty and held him tightly. I guess I would have been scared too. But they didn't have to make such a big deal of it. I knew that day, things would never be the same for me. And that's about true. On the third night after Rusty came home with us, he started a fuss while we were playing Parcheesi.

I was mad at him, God. I didn't care what I said. So I told him, "Mom and Dad love me best because they've had me the longest."

He smarted back, "Yes, but I'm the newest!"

I felt like smacking him. I've been wondering a lot since Rusty came along. Wondering why I was given away as a baby and he was nearly six. Mom explained that children are placed for adoption for different reasons. A good plan is worked out so that the child can have loving parents, enough food, clothes, and toys. I know Mom and Dad love Rusty and me. But I still wonder sometimes. God, you understand what I'm trying to say, don't you? Now that I'm eleven, I worry about lots of things. Why do friends like Beth act the way they do? Why are there teachers like Mrs. Applebonham? Why do I get upset when Mom strongly tells me to clean my room? Why was Grandmother Griffin so upset when I broke her crystal candy dish? Why did I get a dumb brother like Rusty? And yes, God I still wonder why I was given up for adoption.

When Mom commands in her best voice, "Clean your room before going out to play," it doesn't bother me unless it's a wondering day for me.

I guess I love Rusty, except when he makes me mad or when he tattles. One day I wanted to play one of his records. He screamed, "Mom, make her give me my record." Sometimes I wish I had never asked for a brother.

Lucky for me I have other friends besides Beth. She can't decide who is her friend. Friends like Beth are no good for me when I'm wondering.

Why does Mrs. Applebonham have to be so grouchy? Last year, about ten times every day she would peer over her half-moon glasses, rap her desk with a ruler, and yell through her nose, "All right class, get quiet." I even thought about saving a whole week's allowance and buying some vitamins for her. She must feel bad to be so grumpy.

Grandmother Griffin had never fussed at me until the day I broke her candy dish. And that wasn't even my fault. If it hadn't been for that stupid brother of mine, her candy dish would not be broken. Grandmother has always told me I'm her special grandchild. After that happened, I wondered if that is true.

Rusty had snitched a piece of my candy. I wasn't going to let him get away with it. "Ruussty!" I screamed. "Give it back."

"That's for taking my bubble gum yesterday," he shouted.

That did it. I'd been wanting an excuse to whack him since that fuss we had when he tried to win Parcheesi by cheating. He thought because he was new in the family he should get all the attention. He almost does, too, it seems.

I started chasing him around Grandmother's coffee table.

"OK children, stop," called Mom from the kitchen.

"I said stop running," yelled Mom again.

We kept on, just like a merry-go-round. We were both dizzy.

"Children, if you want to run, you must go outside," spoke Grandmother sternly, wiping her hands on her apron as she entered the living room. "I wouldn't want you to get hurt. Besides I'd feel sad if something happened to my candy dish. It was a wedding present to your Great-Grandmother Griffin." She turned toward the kitchen, stopped, looked over her shoulder, and said, "You know, it's quite valuable too."

"Goody-goody," whispered Rusty.

That's how he is about everything, sneaky! Mom told me it's because he feels insecure. She says when he feels good about things he will act differently. Boy, I'll be glad when he feels good about something!

"I'll get you. Wait and see," I told him, pulling my arm back to swing. My right foot caught on the rug. I lost my balance and fell across the coffee table. I went one way, the coffee table and candy dish went another. Rusty giggled.

Mother came rushing into the living room.

"Why did we ever have to get him?" I shouted.

"We wanted another child and thought it would be nice for you to have a brother," she snapped. Half-smiling she said, "Besides, you have brought us so much happiness, we felt another child would add to that happiness."

I guess I'm lucky I wasn't punished.

"You know, Sandi, you have always been special to Dad and me. Rusty is too. Each of you in your own way."

Just then Grandmother walked into the living room, her eyes sadly focused on the shattered glass. "See Sandi, if you had done as I suggested, the candy dish might not be broken." My guilt must have been written on my face. Putting her arms around my shoulders, she said, "But you're worth more to me than all the crystal in the world. Now go play with your brother and forget about the candy dish. Accidents happen." She patted me as I headed for the door.

God, I guess having a brother isn't all bad. Rusty and I often have fun together. Sometimes he acts sort of human. I feel sorry for him when Mom and Dad have to punish him. Maybe it's because I know how he feels. I know he loves me in his own way. I love him, too, although sometimes I wonder.

About a year after Rusty came to live with us, our family was taking a ride in our car. Rusty and I were in the backseat playing ticktacktoe on a cookie box.

Rusty mumbled, "Sandi, give me the box for a minute." Holding his hand over the printing (he couldn't write in cursive then), he printed, "I LOVE YOU, SANDI. DO YOU LOVE ME?"

I took the box from him and began to write.

Mom looked over her shoulder at us. Her eyes spread wide and her forehead wrinkled. I figured she expected me to write, "I hate you, Rusty." The thought did flash through my mind. But I don't feel this way except when we are mad, so I wrote, "YES, I LOVE YOU, RUSTY."

Rusty smiled.

Well, God, we still fuss. But not as often as we did. Mom says we are getting used to each other.

Now we even have serious talks like the time
when . . .

Mom, Rusty, and I were eating dinner at a
restaurant when Dad was out of town on
business. I asked Rusty, "Rusty, who is your real
mother?"
Rusty was sitting next to Mom, and he just
tapped Mom on the shoulder.
I said, "No. Who *borne* you?"
He hunched his shoulders to his neck, stretched
out his arms and hands, palm side up and said, "I
don't know."
"Was it Trudy, Lois, or that other mother you
talk about?" I asked him.

See, God, Rusty lived in three different homes
before he came to ours. I guess Rusty doesn't
wonder as much about this as I do. If he does, he
doesn't talk about it. Maybe boys are like that.
Or maybe he is so happy to have a forever home,
it isn't important to him who *borne* him. I wish I
didn't think so much about it either. I need your
help, God. I seem to wonder more when someone
hurts my feelings, especially Mom or Dad. I
always think if I'm so special, why didn't that
other mother and daddy keep me? If I'm so
special, why does Rusty tattle and why can't Beth
make up her mind who is her best friend? Why

did Grandmother get so upset when I broke her candy dish if I'm her special grandchild? Why does Mom punish me sometimes for not cleaning my room? God, please answer one question for me. Why do I wonder so much? Like . . .

The morning Mom was downstairs fixing breakfast and called upstairs to me, "Sandi, if you don't straighten up your room when you get in from school today, you are restricted for the afternoon."

I waked up that morning in a not-so-good mood. Hearing what Mom said set off my wondering again.

At the breakfast table, Mom asked me if I heard what she told me. All my wondering came out—blam!

"You don't love me," I screamed at her. "You never have, you never will. Nobody loves me! That's why I'm adopted," I yelled. But what I *really* wanted to say was, "I just wonder about my first mother and daddy. Who are they? Where are they? What do they look like? Why did they give me away?" I started crying.

I jumped up, ran to my room, and slammed the door.

Mom followed me. Gently she opened the door and closed it behind her.

"Sandi, why did my telling you to clean your

room cause this outburst?" she asked.

I didn't answer right away. I couldn't stop crying.

It seems that when I'm corrected I feel the most unloved. I wonder if all kids feel this way.

Mom sat on the bed beside me, resting her arm around my drooping shoulders. Something she said made talking to her easier for me and made me *know* I am loved.

She pulled me close to her and spoke softly. "Sandi, when you say I don't love you, no one loves you. . . ." I looked up as she paused and saw her choke back a big lump in her throat. "Are you trying to say that you think you were not loved or that there is something wrong with you? Do you think that is why you were placed for adoption? Do you wonder about your first parents—where they are and what they are like?"

Wow! That made me feel better. Mom knew all along. I didn't have to be the one to say it first. Even better, she wasn't angry with me.

So I answered, "Yes."

"Can we talk about adoption?" she asked.

I nodded my head, "Yes."

"I've thought for some time these things might be troubling you. Perhaps this is why you feel no one likes you. Maybe you even feel unloved. I understand your feelings. Dad and I expect you to have some moments of wondering. These are natural thoughts for you. We know that you love

us. We surely love you. We are not hurt or angry when you ask questions. We only wish we had all the answers. But you must remember you are loved in two ways. Your first parents loved you unselfishly. After talking with an adoption agency and much thought, they worked out a plan for you. Your first parents did this because they wanted what was best for you. Dad and I love you selfishly. We wanted you and love you just because you are you. We will always feel that way. Please remember this," she said. She wiped a tear from her cheek.

So God, I guess that day helped to answer my question. I'll probably still wonder about some things. I may wonder about people like Mrs. Applebonham or friends like Beth. I may wonder why there have to be loudmouthed friends like Debra. I don't suppose I'll ever understand why I have to clean my room so often. Yes, I'll probably wonder again who my first parents are and what they are like. But I don't ever have to wonder again if Mom and Dad understand me and my wondering. I know now that I am loved. But I may still have days I wonder about that again. And I know I am a good person. Oh yes, thank you, God, for answering my question.